W9-CGQ-939

Tugg
and
Teeny

Written by J. Patrick Lewis
Illustrated by Christopher Denise

For Tola with love
—Grandpat

For my friend and comrade of the brush, H.B. Lewis
—Chris

Text Copyright © 2011 J. Patrick Lewis
Illustration Copyright © 2011 Christopher Denise

Sleeping Bear Press™
315 E. Eisenhower Parkway, Suite 200
Ann Arbor, MI 48108
www.sleepingbearpress.com

Sleeping Bear Press is an imprint of Gale, a part of Cengage Learning.

10 9 8 7 6 5 4 3 2 1

Library of Congress Cataloging-in-Publication Data

Lewis, J. Patrick.
Tugg and Teeny / written by J. Patrick Lewis ; illustrated by Christopher Denise.
p. cm.
Summary: Tugg, a gorilla, helps his best friend Teeny, a monkey, in her attempts to become a musi-
cian, an artist, and a poet.
ISBN 978-1-58536-514-2 (case) ISBN 978-1-58536-685-9 (pbk)
[1. Gorilla–Fiction. 2. Monkeys–Fiction. 3. Animals–Fiction. 4. Best friends–Fiction. 5. Friendship–
Fiction.] I. Denise, Christopher, ill. II. Title.
PZ7.L5866Tu 2011
[Fic]–dc22   2010034401

Printed by China Translation & Printing Services Limited, Guangdong
Province, China. 1st printing. 12/2010

Table of Contents

The Strange Stick

"Are you ready for our walk?" asked Tugg.

"Where to, Tugg?" asked Teeny.

"Wherever our twinkle toes take us,"

said Tugg, whistling away.

"Listen!" Teeny said.

She heard the jungle birds sing and sighed, "I wish I could make beautiful music like that."

Teeny looked so sad that Tugg decided he would help his friend get her wish.

In the clearing, Tugg saw BooBoo the baboon hitting a bamboo stick against a tree.

The gorilla called, "What is that, BooBoo? A digging stick?"

"No," said BooBoo, "not sharp enough."

"A drinking straw?"

"It has holes in it, Tugg. It is useless!"

The baboon threw the stick away.

Tugg picked up the stick and looked at it.

He thought for a minute and then laid it on the jungle path where Teeny would be sure to find it.

"Hey, Tugg, what is this?" Teeny asked.

"Maybe Violet will know," said Tugg.

"Warthogs are very smart."

"Violet," said Tugg, "what is this piece
of wood?"

"A backscratcher for a lion," said Violet.

"Lions just roll in the dirt when they
want to scratch an itch," Teeny said.

Teeny pointed the stick to the sky and looked through it.

"What could it be?" she wondered.

"Try blowing on the end and see what happens," said Tugg.

Teeny blew. Squeak, squawk, screech.

"I like it!" Teeny said. "Someday,

Tuggboat, I will be like the birds and make

beautiful music on this stick."

Tugg knew that Teeny was a monkey

who thought she could do anything she set

her mind to.

"Of course you will, Monkeyface."

Back home, they took turns cleaning house and cooking meals.

But in the evenings, Teeny went deep into the jungle to practice on her stick.

At first she could only squeak. But as the weeks passed, her squeaks turned into peeps, and the peeps turned into tweets and toodles.

Soon the jungle went to sleep each

night to the soothing sounds from Teeny's

stick.

One morning Teeny and Tugg were

awakened by loud noises. They ran outside.

"Surprise!" the whole neighborhood

shouted. "We want to make beautiful

music, too. Will you teach us?"

After hearing Teeny practice on her stick each night, all the animals had decided to take music lessons. Even Tugg joined in.

And that is how beautiful music came to the jungle.

What's in a Picture?

"Look!" said Tugg.

"What is it?" asked Teeny.

"Paintings," said Tugg.

"Painting is for the birds," said Teeny.

"Yes, painting *is* for the birds. And for the reptiles, the big cats, the …"

"I hope it is not boring," Teeny grumbled.

Teeny stopped at the first two pictures.

Her mouth fell open.

"They are fabulous!" she said. "And look at this one, Tugg. Can you believe it?" Teeny shouted. "It is *us!* Violet painted us."

"That was very nice of her," said the

gorilla.

Teeny ran into the Jungle Visitors' Shop

and bought paint and art supplies.

"We must hurry home, Tuggboat,"

said Teeny.

Teeny set up her easel and

started to work.

She had been painting for a whole

week when Chuckie Cheetah ran by.

"What does this painting look like?"

the monkey asked him.

"A swamp," said Chuckie.

Teeny frowned.

Zig and Zag, the wacky Zebra brothers, trotted over.

"What am I painting?" Teeny asked them.

"Purple weeds," said Zig.

"Grouchy Zig waking up," said Zag.

Teeny groaned.

A month had gone by when Margie Barge waddled over.

"Since you are an art expert, Margie," said Teeny, "tell me what I am painting."

Margie Barge stared at the picture for a long time. "Ah yes," she said. "Five divided by twelve."

Teeny was almost in tears.

"What is wrong, Teeny?" Tugg asked.

"No one can guess what my painting is!"

"I know what it is, Monkeyface," said

Tugg, "and I think it is beautiful. But we

should ask Violet her opinion. She is an

artist too, remember."

Teeny and Tugg had already thanked Violet for her "Best Friends" painting in the Animal Art Show.

"Of course," said Teeny, "Violet will know right away."

"Please look at Teeny's painting, Violet, and tell us if you recognize it," said Tugg.

He winked at Violet. He winked again.

Violet saw Tugg winking. She saw the hopeful look in Teeny's eyes.

She took a long look at the painting that was on Teeny's easel.

Then Violet said tearfully, "Monkeyface, how can I ever thank you for this gorgeous portrait of, of...*ME!*"

Teeny's Poem

Teeny and Tugg were enjoying the

afternoon on their front porch.

"I finally finished my poem," said

Teeny, very pleased with herself.

Tugg put on his reading glasses.

He read the poem. It did not take long.

The bees buzz,
the birds sing.
The End

"Short and sweet, Monkeyface."

"Yes," said the monkey. "Good poets get right to the point."

"Let's ask Violet what she thinks," said Tugg. "Warthogs are poetry experts."

"She will love my poem," said Teeny.

"Violet," asked Tugg, "what do you think of this poem?"

The warthog burped, and then read the poem.

"Where is the next page?" she asked.

Teeny wanted to cry.

Violet said, "Be thankful that it is not *your* poem, Teeny."

"But it IS my poem, Violet!"

"Oops," said Violet.

"Hmm," said Tugg. "Here is an idea. Why not spend some time thinking about your poem, Monkeyface?"

So for three whole days, Teeny thought about her poem.

She climbed up a tree to gaze at the moon.

She sat at her desk with her notebook scribbling ~~crossing off~~ scribbling ~~crossing off.~~

This was hard work that seemed to take forever.

On the fourth day, she shouted, "Tuggboat! Now I really *am* finished."

Throughout the jungle, the gorilla's voice boomed.

"Attention, everyone! Come and hear Teeny read her new poem!"

Teeny was very nervous.

She read her new poem slowly.

Bees buzz,
birds sing

The jungle fell silent.

Teeny whispered to Tugg, "I took out

the two *the*'s. Isn't it magical?"

Tugg was about to congratulate his

little friend when suddenly…

The tiger roared, "*Brilliant!*"

The giraffe cried, "*Fabulous!*"

"Can we hear *more?*" begged the baboon.

Teeny blushed. "I was saving the best

part for last."

Bees buzz,

birds sing

warthogs burp...

and gorillas glow.

Every animal started hooting and

clapping wildly!

"AUTHOR!
AUTHOR!"

"Monkeyface," said Tugg, "you are on

your way to becoming a good writer."

"Thanks to you, Tuggboat," Teeny said.

"What should I write about tomorrow?" asked Teeny.

"Write about what you know best," Tugg replied.

The monkey thought and thought.

Then she wrote down the title for her new poem, "What It Means To Have a Best Friend."